Secret Cargo

NANCY DREW®/THE HARDY BOYS®

Be a Detective Mystery Stories™

#4

Secret Cargo

by
**Carolyn Keene and
Franklin W. Dixon**

Illustrated by
Paul Frame

WANDERER BOOKS
Published by Simon & Schuster, Inc., New York

Published by WANDERER BOOKS
A Division of Simon & Schuster, Inc.
Simon & Schuster Building
1230 Avenue of the Americas
New York, New York 10020

Designed by Stanley S. Drate

Manufactured in the United States of America

10 9 8 7 6 5 4 3 2

WANDERER and colophon are registered trademarks
of Simon & Schuster, Inc.

NANCY DREW, NANCY DREW MYSTERY STORIES
and THE HARDY BOYS are trademarks of
Stratemeyer Syndicate, registered in the United States
Patent and Trademark Office.
BE A DETECTIVE MYSTERY STORIES is a
trademark of Stratemeyer Syndicate.

Library of Congress Cataloging in Publication Data

Keene, Carolyn.
  Secret cargo.

  (Nancy Drew/the Hardy boys be a detective mystery
stories ; #4)
  Summary: Nancy Drew and the Hardy brothers run into
danger when they try to prevent the sabotage of an anti-
pollution campaign. The reader controls the outcome of
the story by choosing different ways of advancing the
plot.
  1. Plot-it-yourself stories. [1. Mystery and detective
stories. 2. Plot-it-yourself stories] I. Dixon, Franklin W.
II. Title. III. Series: Keene, Carolyn. Nancy Drew/the
Hardy boys be a detective mystery stories ; 4.
PZ7.K23Sc 1984   [Fic]   83-23302
ISBN 0-671-49922-X

Dear Fans,

Since so many of you have written to us saying how much you want to be detectives like Nancy Drew and The Hardy Boys, we figured out a way. Of course, we had to put our heads together to create mysteries that were so baffling they needed help from everyone, including Nancy, Frank, Joe, and you!

In these exciting new BE A DETECTIVE MYS-TERY STORIES you'll be part of a great team of amateur sleuths following clues and wily suspects. At every turn you'll have a chance to pick a different trail filled with adventure that may lead to danger, surprise, or an amazing discovery!

The choices are all yours—see how many there are and have fun!

C.K. and F.W.D.

What a wonderful day to be alive! Nancy Drew mused as she drove her beloved blue sports sedan on the highway just outside of River Heights. Her titian-blond hair streamed in the wind blowing through the open window. River Heights's famous girl detective was in grand spirits. She'd recently solved a complex case with her good friends Frank and Joe Hardy of Bayport, and she looked forward to working with them again. Mysteries have a way of showing up when you least expect them, Nancy thought. You never know when something extraordinary will happen.

Suddenly, a huge silver-and-black truck raced alongside her small car, its exhausts roaring like thunder.

Even though the rig was in the next lane, it seemed to come dangerously close to her. Nancy's hands tightened on the wheel as she moved farther to the right to let the huge truck pass. She saw the River Heights exit ahead of her and drove off the highway. The truck barreled past at high speed.

"Whew!" Nancy gasped. "He almost sideswiped me. Didn't he realize how close he was?" She glanced at the highway. Trailing the speeding truck as if linked to it by an invisible cord was a black sedan. In it were three men wearing dark hats.

Turn to page 3

3

Was that car chasing the truck? Nancy wondered as she drove toward her lovely brick home. When she arrived, Hannah Gruen, the Drews' kindly housekeeper, was waving to her from the front porch.

"Come on, Nancy, I have a nice lunch waiting for you," the woman called.

Nancy's mind was still on the truck as she sipped iced tea and nibbled a crisp green salad in the backyard. But her concern was finally forgotten with the arrival of her two best friends, Bess Marvin and George Fayne. Both girls were breathless with excitement.

"Guess what!" Bess exclaimed, pulling up a chair to the garden table. Her eyes were on a bowl of freshly picked strawberries sprinkled with sugar.

Nancy chuckled. "Help yourself, Bess," she offered. "As for guessing what, I give up."

George took the other chair. Her tall, tomboyish good looks contrasted with chubby Bess's blond femininity. "Chris Todd is giving a folk-song concert in River Heights," she announced.

"And we've got tickets for all of us!" Bess added.

Turn to next page

4

"Chris Todd isn't just a famous folk singer," George said. "He's also the best-known environmentalist in the whole country."

Nancy's smile turned to a frown. "Unfortunately, he's also one of the most hated. There are a number of people who would like to see his efforts to protect our environment stopped at any cost."

The phone rang as Hannah refilled the strawberry bowl. Nancy answered it. When she rejoined her friends, her face was grim.

"What happened?" George inquired anxiously.

Nancy sat down. "A huge truck nearly sideswiped me this morning," she stated. "That phone call was from the driver. He wants to see me immediately."

"We'll come with you," George offered.

Nancy told her friends what she had found out as they drove off in her blue sedan. "The driver's name is Layne Griffin. He insisted that I meet him at the River Heights truck stop. He said he was being chased!"

"Who was chasing him?" George asked suspiciously.

Nancy shrugged. "I don't know. But we'll find out in a minute. There's the River Heights truck stop. And there's his truck."

Turn to next page

5

Layne Griffin, a good-looking young man of twenty, was sitting nervously in a booth in the small restaurant when the girls entered. He introduced himself and profusely apologized for the fright he'd given Nancy earlier.

"I'm a driver for my father's trucking company," he explained. "Some men hired us recently to carry some cargo. My truck is sealed until I reach my destination, and I have a feeling there's something illegal about it. Somehow these people acted . . . strange."

"So you'd like me to investigate, is that it?" Nancy inquired. She realized that she was about to embark on another case and was eager to begin. Layne Griffin appeared to be a sincere young man whose troubled face was filled with trust.

"Yes," Layne responded. "I've got to know who's behind this, what I'm carrying, and what it's all about."

"Have you spoken with the police?" Nancy asked.

Layne shook his head. "No," he whispered, glancing through the window at his silver-and-black truck outside. "You see, I'm being followed. If I go to the authorities, those people might harm me or our company. Will you help me?"

Nancy nodded reassuringly. "Yes," she replied. "I'll do my best. Where are you delivering the cargo?"

Turn to next page

6

But before he had a chance to answer, Layne leaped up from the table. "I'll be right back," he said, and ran to the door leading to the telephones.

The girls waited patiently, though Nancy was apprehensive about his sudden departure. Her suspicions were confirmed when the roar of the big truck suddenly filled the restaurant. The Griffin Motorways rig was speeding out of the parking lot!

Nancy ran to her car, followed by Bess and George, but it was blocked by a confused motorist trying to park. By the time the tangle of autos was undone, the truck was gone. "I can't even be certain which direction it went," Nancy lamented, looking at a major intersection of highways a short distance away.

George stared at the spot where the truck had been parked. Her eyes lighted on a piece of paper on the ground. "Look, Nancy," she said, as she picked it up. "This could have fallen out of Layne's truck."

Nancy stared at the paper. On it was a single word.

Turn to page 7

7

"Greenglobe," she read aloud.

"That's the name of Chris Todd's clean environment campaign," George pointed out.

"It's also the name of his magnificent sailboat he uses to publicize it," Bess added.

Nancy nodded. "And you know what? The *Greenglobe* was recently in Bayport, where Frank and Joe Hardy live. I think I'll give them a call. Perhaps they can help."

To get Frank and Joe into the investigation now, turn to page 8.
To decide where the Hardys will pick up the investigation, turn to page 9.

8

Nancy immediately phoned the famous detective brothers. "I could use your help," she concluded after she'd explained what had happened.

"Sure, Nancy," Frank said. "We can be in River Heights by tonight."

That evening, the Hardys and the Drews sat down to a marvelous dinner served by Hannah Gruen.

"There isn't much to go on," Nancy said as they discussed the case. "All I know is that Layne Griffin is afraid of these people who hired his truck."

Carson Drew, a well-known lawyer, spoke up. "He may have good reason to be afraid. The fact that he bolted out of the restaurant without another word indicates he saw something or someone that was threatening to him."

Frank nodded. "And then there's the possible connection to Chris Todd's environmental program."

"Or his sailboat," Joe added. "The word 'Greenglobe' could mean either."

To pursue Layne's disappearance, turn to page 10.
To pursue the environmental connection,
turn to page 14.
To pursue the sailboat clue, turn to page 15.

9

Frank Hardy answered the phone. "Of course we know the *Greenglobe*," he said, responding to Nancy's question. "In fact, we visited her at the dock in Bayport Harbor just recently."

Nancy explained the mysterious circumstances surrounding Layne Griffin, the secret cargo, and the other strange events of the day.

Frank stroked his chin as he turned to his younger brother, Joe. "There's something peculiar going on which may involve Chris Todd," he stated. "Nancy would like us to enter this case—"

Joe nodded firmly. "Of course," he said. "We'll be glad to."

To accompany Frank and Joe to River Heights, turn to page 11.
To investigate the mystery with the Hardys in Bayport, turn to page 12.

10

Early the next morning the three investigators called Layne Griffin's company and asked to speak to him. They were told that he had not checked in since the previous afternoon.

"Maybe we can find out from one of the truck stops in the area where he went," Nancy suggested, and the friends got into her car and began making the rounds. After visiting a dozen places, they got their first break at a small fuel stop called Fillerup.

"Griffin Motorways?" a craggy old gent said in response to their questions. "Just had one here this mornin'. Young fella drivin'. Bought fuel and took off like he was carryin' fresh fish, if you know what I mean. He was in a hurry."

"This morning!" Joe exclaimed. "Then we can't be far behind him."

The old man cocked his head. "You're the second ones today been askin' about him," he said.

The sleuths stared at one another. "Who else did?" Frank inquired.

The old man scratched his head. "Don't rightly know. Just some men wearin' hats and drivin' a black sedan," he replied.

"Then somebody *is* following Layne," Nancy declared as she turned the blue sports sedan back onto the highway to pursue the increasingly warm trail of Layne Griffin. "But who?"

Turn to page 18

11

The Hardys flew to River Heights early the next morning. When they arrived, they went to the airport's waiting room, where Nancy eagerly greeted them. She was alone. A deep frown covered her face.

"There's been a new development in the case," she announced as the three friends walked out into the parking lot. "Layne Griffin has disappeared. After his sudden departure yesterday, I called Griffin Motorways. They told me Layne failed to report in as he was instructed to do every day. They don't know where he is."

"Where was he going?" Joe asked.

"Nobody knows, not even his company," she replied. "Apparently the people who hired Griffin Motorways are so secretive they only told Layne where he was to deliver the cargo."

Turn to page 13

12

"We'll be glad to help you, Nancy," Frank said into the mouthpiece. "The first thing we'll do is check out the *Greenglobe*. She's still in Bayport, you know."

Frank and Joe drove straight to the harbor to investigate the magnificent 125-foot sailboat, which was docked alongside a broad public pier so visitors could board her.

Her glistening white hull and brass brightwork sparkled in the sun beneath three tall spruce masts adorned with a myriad of ropes and lines looking like giant spider webs. "She's a beauty," Joe commented as he parked the car.

"She's a perfect replica of a boat that sailed these waters a hundred years ago," Frank added as he and his younger brother approached the elegant craft. "The original was used to haul cargo up and down the coast."

"What could Layne Griffin and his secret cargo have to do with this boat?" Joe wondered aloud.

"Let's board her and see what we can learn," Frank suggested. "We won't look suspicious if we mingle with the other tourists."

Turn to page 17

Without delay, the determined young investigators got on the trail of the missing young trucker and his huge rig filled with unknown cargo.

13

"He's less than a day ahead of us," Nancy stated as her blue sedan hummed over the highway in the direction Layne was traveling when he passed Nancy the day before.

"We'll have to check every eating place in the area," Joe suggested. "Maybe someone will remember seeing him."

"Wherever he is, it's going to take some good old-fashioned gumshoe detective work to find him," Nancy concluded.

Hours later, with no luck yet, the detectives drove into the fifth truck stop.

Turn to page 16

14

"We can start investigating the environmental angle right here," Nancy offered. "Todd's giving a concert in River Heights this evening. Bess, George, and I already have tickets. We'll get two more and we'll all go."

"Excellent!" Frank and Joe exclaimed.

That night the five friends sat under the stars on a blanket in the park as Chris Todd and his group performed for the benefit of Greenglobe, Todd's environmental-awareness program.

Nancy tapped George Fayne on the shoulder. "May I borrow your glasses?" she whispered. Then she pointed the small binoculars at the group's drummer, a portly fellow with a round face, and began sketching on the back of her program. Her artist's fingers flew as she created a perfect likeness of him on the paper.

Bess Marvin watched with amusement. "What do you find so interesting about the drummer?"

Nancy put a finishing touch to the portrait she'd drawn. "I saw him at the truck stop this morning just before Layne Griffin disappeared."

Turn to page 25

The next morning Mr. Drew was watching the news in the den. A few moments later he rushed into the living room, where the young people were discussing what to do next.

"Come, quick!" he called out. "There's an item on the news that will interest you. Chris Todd has just announced he's canceling the rest of his tour!"

"What!" the Hardys and Nancy cried in disbelief.

"Not only that," Mr. Drew went on, "but he's also planning to put the *Greenglobe* up for sale and will dismiss her crew."

The young people followed Mr. Drew to the comfortable den, where the television newscaster was just ending his surprising story. "Todd has declined an interview," he concluded.

"It doesn't make any sense at all to plan a huge national tour to promote a clean environment, and then suddenly drop out in the middle," Frank said.

Nancy was grim. She'd looked forward to the concert, of course. But more important to her was the fact that a powerful voice against pollution had been mysteriously stilled.

Hannah Gruen entered the room. "There's a telephone call for you, Nancy," she said. "It's from a Mr. Layne Griffin."

Turn to page 22

16

As the blue sedan entered the parking lot, Nancy's quick eyes spotted something familiar. "That car!" she exclaimed.

A man wearing a hat pulled far down over his face sat in the black sedan Nancy pointed out to Frank and Joe. "That's the one I saw following Layne's truck yesterday," she added.

As she spoke, the car started up and turned onto the highway. Nancy followed it at a safe distance to avoid being detected. "The only difference is, there were three men in it yesterday," she told the boys.

"If your observation is correct, I have a strong feeling that guy is going to lead us to the others," Joe said.

Frank spoke up. "And if my hunch is correct, he's also going to lead us to something else."

To follow Joe's hunch, turn to page 19.
To pursue Frank's, turn to page 20.

They wandered about the boat's polished teak decks like ordinary visitors. But their keen detective instincts were tuned to look for anything that might link the *Greenglobe* to Layne Griffin, his unknown cargo, and the mystery of why he had suddenly disappeared after talking to Nancy Drew in River Heights that very morning.

After inspecting every nook and cranny, the sleuths reached the last place they hadn't investigated, a sail locker at the end of a narrow passageway below decks.

"We've covered every inch of this boat without finding a single clue," Joe complained. He jiggled the handle, but the door to the locker would not budge. "I don't think there are any clues on the *Greenglobe*."

"We can't leave without making sure," Frank insisted, even though he was just as discouraged as his brother. He bowed his head in intense concentration, determined to think of something to do next, when his eyes caught the faint glimmer of something sticking out from under the door.

Turn to page 23

18

A few miles down the road, Nancy glanced into her rear-view mirror. "Oh, oh," she gulped. A black-and-white state-police car was behind her with its red light flashing. She immediately pulled to the side.

A smiling officer sauntered over to her. "Don't worry, Miss Drew," he said through the open window, "you didn't break the speed limit. This message for you was found at a truck stop this morning." He handed her a folded sheet of paper, then said good-bye and left.

Nancy read the hastily scrawled note aloud. "Am being followed by men in black sedan. Suspect they want my cargo. Meet me at 66 tonight. Layne."

"66?" Joe said with a puzzled look. "What's that?"

"May I see the note?" Frank asked, taking the paper from Nancy. Then he gasped. Layne's message was written on the back of a flyer announcing Chris Todd's concert tour!

To pursue the 66 clue, turn to page 28.
To investigate the flyer, turn to page 34.

A short drive later, the detectives stopped and hid themselves in a thicket of bushes near an abandoned farmhouse where they had followed the black sedan and its lone driver. A large red barn sat in the open farmyard a short distance behind the house.

Nancy watched through the powerful binoculars she kept inside her car's glove compartment. "Nothing's moved since the man went into that house," she whispered.

"I'd like to get a look at that barn," Joe volunteered.

"That's an excellent idea," Frank rejoined. "In the meantime, Nancy and I'll investigate the house."

To follow Joe, turn to page 24.
To go with Frank and Nancy, turn to page 27.

20

"Where do you think he's going?" Nancy asked as the three secretly drove behind the black sedan into a deeply wooded area of low hills.

"If that's the car that was tailing Layne, my hunch is that it's still following him," Frank said.

No sooner had he spoken than they rounded a corner and came to a secluded clearing. In the center of the open area stood Layne's truck, the black sedan, and a towering pile of battered and leaking oil drums.

"An illegal toxic-waste dump!" Nancy gasped.

The sleuths carefully hid their car and circled back to the dump without being seen.

Nancy pointed to Layne's huge truck. A man sat in the cab behind the steering wheel. "It's Layne!" the girl said in a low tone.

Joe shaded his eyes as he studied the silent, unmoving figure. "He's tied up. I'll bet he was on to their scheme."

Turn to page 26

22

Frank and Joe gathered around Nancy, who held the receiver so they could hear, too. On the other end, Layne spoke anxiously. "I'm being watched. I'm in Bayport, where I delivered my cargo to the *Greenglobe*."

"The *Greenglobe* is back there?" Nancy asked.

"Yes. But there's danger—somebody coming—phone booth, Pier Six, look up—" Then the line went dead.

The sleuths stared at one another. They had heard the desperate voice of someone in obvious danger, yet they were helpless to do anything about it!

Joe quickly committed the sketchy clues to paper. "But what does it mean?" he asked.

"Pier Six is where the *Greenglobe* must be docked. That's where she was before," Frank said.

"We have to go to Bayport immediately," Nancy spoke up. "Let me call the airport."

After a short conversation, her face dropped and she hung up the telephone. "We can't get a commercial flight out until tomorrow," she said. "I've rented a plane, but it won't be available until six."

The young detectives were unhappy about the delay, but there was nothing they could do. At six o'clock sharp, they were at the airport.

Turn to page 32

Frank quickly dropped to his knees and pried it loose. It was part of a shipping label, the kind pasted on large cartons before transport. Even though it was only a piece of the original sticker, he was able to make out the sender. "Griffin Motorways!" he read.

"Then there *is* a connection between Layne and the *Greenglobe!*" Joe declared.

23

Turn to page 49

24

Joe sneaked through the woods to the barn and cupped his ear to listen. Silent as a tomb, he thought. He sniffed the air. There's a truck in the barn, he concluded. Big rigs have a distinct odor of rubber and oil, and that's what I smell right now.

The young sleuth peeked into the barn through a dusty window. His deduction was correct. Inside was a silver-and-black Griffin Motorways truck. Another rig was parked next to it. Joe pried open the window and climbed in. He had only gone a few steps when he froze. Gruff men's voices broke the eerie silence.

"Did you finish transferring the cargo to our truck?" one man asked.

"Yes," another answered. "The crates are all loaded."

There was some noise that drowned out further conversation. But Joe managed to pick up some words. "Bermuda—final destination—pickup—get Griffin rig back on the road."

"It'll be picked up. Don't worry about it. Just take the empty Griffin rig back on the road and get our truck on the way."

They've hijacked Layne's cargo to their own truck, Joe thought. I have to tell Frank and Nancy.

Turn to page 30

At intermission, Frank, Joe, George, and Bess gathered around Nancy. "Do you mean you believe Chris Todd's drummer has something to do with Layne Griffin's secret cargo?" Joe asked.

"I don't know," she responded. "But I do know he's the same person I saw at the truck stop this morning."

"It could be a coincidence," Bess said. "After all, Chris Todd's group *is* in River Heights."

"I know," Nancy replied. "But the word 'coincidence' bothers me in any investigation."

The others nodded agreement.

"I think it would be a good idea to talk to Chris Todd," Joe suggested. "He may be able to tell us something."

Nancy wrote a note requesting an interview and gave it to a security guard to deliver to Chris Todd.

"Of course I'll talk to those famous young investigators and their friends," the folk singer said after his performance, as the youths were ushered into his dressing room. He greeted everyone, then listened with interest while Nancy and the Hardys explained their latest case.

Turn to page 38

26

Four men suddenly appeared from behind the truck. "The three wearing dark hats are the ones I saw following Layne," Nancy whispered. "But who's the guy in the white officer's cap?"

Joe slapped his palm against his forehead. "Officer!" he nearly shouted. "He's the captain of the *Greenglobe*. Frank and I saw him when we visited her in Bayport. What's he doing here?"

The investigators listened as the men's conversation drifted from the clearing.

"We'll make it look like an accident," one said to the *Greenglobe*'s captain. "You tell the newspapers you saw smoke from the highway as you were driving to see your boss, Chris Todd. Say you found the burning truck crashed into this toxic-waste dump and that you tried to save the driver, but it was too late. That'll make you a double hero, and you'll get us all twice the publicity you would have if you'd only found the fake dump the way we originally planned before this nosy driver decided to uncover our scheme."

"Todd won't dare fire me now, and your agency will make a fortune selling tickets to his concerts!" the captain laughed.

Turn to page 31

Frank and Nancy dashed across the farmyard to the house. An open door led to the basement from where they heard a low moan.

"It came from there," Frank whispered, pointing down the stairway.

Exercising great caution, the sleuths descended the steps. The moans continued, growing louder as Frank and Nancy advanced toward the warren of small rooms beneath the old house. They stopped at a door hanging loosely from its hinges. Frank put his ear to it and gestured with his thumb. "In here," he said.

Nancy brushed away cobwebs that clung like thin strands of glue to her titian-blond hair and opened the door. "It's Layne Griffin!" she gasped.

Turn to page 29

28

Nancy, Frank, and Joe pored over the strange message as they sat in the car at the side of the highway. "66? 66? 66?" Nancy repeated over and over. "What could it mean?"

Joe was studying a map of the area. "There aren't any roads numbered 66 around here," he declared. Then, with a flash of inspiration, he grinned.

"Maybe it's not a 66," he declared.

"What do you mean?" Frank asked.

"It could also mean GG," Joe said. "Layne wrote it in a hurry and it's not very clear—"

"You're right!" Nancy cried out. "And I'll bet it's short for *Greenglobe*. Maybe Layne wants us to meet him at Chris Todd's sailboat!"

"The *Greenglobe* is returning to Bayport tomorrow after visiting several smaller towns up the coast," Joe said excitedly.

The young people quickly drove back to River Heights. Early next morning they boarded a flight to Bayport, where Frank and Joe's car was waiting for them in the long-term parking lot. They found out that a concert was scheduled by Chris Todd and his group at the harbor that night.

Turn to page 36

Layne was lying in a moldy corner. An ugly red lump glistened on his forehead. Frank quickly untied the unfortunate young trucker. "I'm Frank Hardy," he explained. "What happened?"

Layne shook his head groggily, then smiled at Nancy. "When I saw the men in the restaurant, I thought I could ditch them and call you later, but they caught up with me. They're after my cargo."

"Do you know what it is?" Nancy asked.

"No. Only that its destination is the *Greenglobe*. I started to write a note, but they saw me."

"The clue I found," Nancy exclaimed.

A sudden loud shout from outside galvanized the youths' attention. "It's Joe," Frank exclaimed. "He needs help."

He bounded up the cellar steps with Nancy and Layne in his wake. When they reached the front door, they halted abruptly and looked out at the barn. It was a raging inferno with flames soaring high into the sky!

"Where's Joe?" Nancy screamed.

Frank shook his head in despair. "I don't know!"

Turn to page 37

30

He retraced his steps to the window and began to hoist himself up. Suddenly, his hands slipped on the sill and he hit the floor with a thud.

A chill went up Joe's spine. Quickly, he grabbed the sill again, hoping that no one had heard.

If you think Joe makes it out safely, turn to page 45.
If you think Joe was heard, turn to page 51.

"So that's it," Nancy said. "It's a scam to create fake publicity to sell concert tickets and keep Todd from firing the *Greenglobe*'s captain."

"The truck!" Joe gasped.

Layne had untied his bonds and started the truck. It roared toward the men with its exhausts belching and horns blowing.

"Now's our chance," Frank called. He and the others burst from their hiding place to grab the terrified men. With skillful karate chops, the youths quickly captured the plotters.

They unraveled the scheme after turning the criminals over to the police. "The gang shipped drums of toxic waste to a dump site for the captain to 'discover,'" Frank said. "The publicity would increase ticket sales for concerts and would make it impossible for Todd to fire the captain, which for some reason he was planning to do."

"Layne's suspicion got Nancy into the case, but before he could talk to her, his shadows appeared at the truck stop," Joe continued.

"I thought I could ditch them," Layne explained. "But they knew I was on to them and decided to capture me and use my truck in their scheme. Luckily I had heard them mention Greenglobe, and the clue I left for Nancy convinced her to call you two and continue the investigation."

"Which is now officially ended," Nancy added with a smile.

END

32

While Nancy piloted their sleek rented airplane from River Heights to Bayport, Joe pulled out his notes and studied the clues they'd gathered in the complex case.

"This is how it stacks up," he said, referring to his notes. "Todd was in the middle of a national tour to promote a clean environment. The River Heights concert was still scheduled as late as yesterday, or perhaps even this morning. Layne tried to talk to Nancy yesterday, but someone or something scared him away. She found a one-word clue, Greenglobe. Layne mentioned that someone was following him. He didn't know what his cargo was. Those are the facts."

"My conclusion," Frank said, "is that Layne's cargo has something to do with Chris Todd's sudden decision to halt the campaign."

"We'll soon find out if you're right," Nancy said. "There are the lights of Bayport now."

Turn to next page

Before making their landing at the airport, Nancy banked the plane sharply to fly over the harbor. Lights sparkled against the black water of the big bay, but because it was night, there was very little boat traffic.

"The sailboat docking area is directly below us," Frank shouted over the hum of the engine. "Pier Six should be—"

"*Greenglobe* is gone!" Joe exclaimed in disbelief. "Her slip is empty!"

Nancy made a low pass over the sailboat berths. The 125-foot *Greenglobe* was nowhere in sight.

"Maybe we can locate her from the air," she suggested.

"We might have better luck looking for clues at Pier Six," Joe offered.

"Just tell me where you want to go and I'll get you there," Nancy said as she leveled the plane and waited for directions.

To search for **Greenglobe** *from the air, turn to page 43.*
To land and investigate Pier Six, turn to page 47.

34

The sleuths pulled into the next truck stop and ordered sodas at the counter. Joe pored over an open road map as Frank and Nancy studied the flyer with the brief cryptic message.

"I thought 66 might be a highway near here," Joe said. "But there's no such number."

A man at the end of the counter chuckled. "I guess you'd have to be a trucker to know 66," he said, putting down a steaming cup of black coffee. "Let me show you."

He traced his finger over the map. "This here's *State* highway number 6," he explained, "and this is *U.S.* highway number 6. Where they come together, us truckers call that 66."

The sleuths thanked the man enthusiastically and were on the road again in minutes. "If Layne's at 66 as I think he'll be, the first thing I want to ask him is what connection this Chris Todd concert announcement has to do with his case," Nancy said.

Turn to next page

A busy diner stood at the intersection of the two highways. When Nancy entered its parking lot, she pointed to a weatherworn sign above the gate that said, 66 DINER.

"That's the biggest clue we've tracked down so far," she chuckled.

"No, it's not," Joe said. "That is." He pointed to a corner of the lot, where Layne Griffin's truck sat, its cab empty.

Nancy quickly parked the blue sedan and the three investigators entered the diner. Nancy's eyes opened wide.

Sitting at the counter, staring straight at her, was Layne Griffin! His face was impassive and he ignored her completely. Her instincts warned her not to greet him. Instead, her quick eyes darted around the small room looking for the reason for Layne's cool attitude. She spotted it immediately. Three grim-faced men were seated in a rear booth, watching the young man like hawks.

Layne casually got up and paid for his meal, brushing by the young detectives as he made his way to the exit. His shadows followed.

"That was Layne," Nancy whispered to the Hardys when they were gone. "He's being tailed by those men."

Turn to page 48

36

At seven that evening, the sleuths arrived at the dock as the *Greenglobe* was just pulling in. A Dixieland band played jazz for a crowd gathered at the wharf, creating a festive mood.

"I wonder what connection the *Greenglobe* has to Layne's secret cargo?" Joe commented as he, Frank, and Nancy scanned the area for signs of the missing young trucker.

"We'll know soon enough," Frank interjected. "From your description of him, Nancy, I think that fellow over there may be Layne Griffin."

Nancy's eyes followed Frank's. They lighted on a dark-haired man with a muscular build who was quietly circling the concert audience as if looking for someone.

"That's him," she acknowledged. "I'd recognize that strong chin and broad brow anywhere."

"He may still be followed," Joe cautioned as the sleuths moved to meet the writer of the mysterious note. "I suggest we be careful."

Turn to page 40

The three ran toward the flaming structure. Just then Joe appeared in a low window that was still untouched by the fire. "Stop them!" he shouted and pointed to three men who came running out the door with their clothes smoking, calling for help.

Joe climbed out the window and leaped in their direction, knocking one to the ground. Frank and Layne ran to assist him. In seconds, the criminals were captured, shivering with fear like frightened chickens.

"The secret cargo was paint," Joe explained. "It was for the *Greenglobe*. These guys were mixing a deadly poison in it so wherever the boat went, it would kill hundreds of fish. That would destroy Chris Todd's credibility as an environmentalist. These people are in the toxic-waste disposal business and I heard them say Todd's campaign was creating too much public awareness. What they didn't know was the stuff they put in the paint would make it explode at a certain temperature. It got so hot in the barn that it just blew up!"

Local firemen and policemen appeared in time to save Layne's truck and to cart the plotters off to jail. The sleuths and their new friend made plans to return to River Heights and tell Chris Todd about the scheme that might have ruined his public image.

END

38

"I'm afraid I can't help you regarding Mr. Layne Griffin's suspicions about his cargo," he said when they were finished. "But I can assure you that Billy John, my drummer, was only doing his job. He travels ahead of the group to make certain our concert arrangements are in order."

Later, over ice cream at a soda shop, the five friends pondered the thin lead they had discovered.

"It looks like Billy John's presence at the truck stop was a coincidence after all," Bess Marvin concluded.

Nancy was doodling over the perfect sketch she'd made of the drummer. "I guess so," she said, sounding unconvinced.

Joe Hardy had been very quiet. He was studying his program and surveyed a list of the towns where Chris Todd's group was scheduled to perform. "I think I've uncovered something very interesting," he said suddenly. "Each of the places on this list has recently had a toxic-waste-dump problem."

Turn to next page

"They had?" George asked curiously.

"No one knew River Heights had a dump site until one was discovered just a week ago, according to a newspaper article I read before dinner," Joe went on. "The article said a fly-by-night operation was found in a nearby woods where twenty barrels of dangerous pollutants were found. They were cleaned up in a day and there haven't been any problems since."

Nancy looked at the list. "Westbury Center . . . Doddville . . . Freehoke," she read aloud. "I don't know all of these places, but Westbury Center and Doddville aren't far from here—and they also just reported secret toxic-waste dumping within the last week."

The excited group pored over the list lying on the table. Frank put into words what they all had on their minds. "Each town where Chris Todd is playing a concert promoting a clean environment has just uncovered a toxic-waste dump. That's much more than a coincidence. That's a clue!"

Turn to page 55

40

Layne walked cautiously around the edge of the crowd. When he spotted Nancy, he came toward her, but suddenly she froze and signaled him with her eyes to stay where he was.

"What's the matter?" Joe asked.

"I just noticed two men in the audience who are not watching the band," Nancy whispered. "They seem to be watching Layne instead."

"Tell you what," Frank suggested. "You walk away from here. Layne will follow you, and we in turn will follow his shadows, if that's what they are."

"Good idea!" Nancy grinned and slowly started to stroll away from the dock. She looked at Layne, and he got the message. He went after her.

Frank and Joe waited a few seconds. Then they saw the two men, hats pulled low over their eyes, getting up from the back row and trailing the pair.

Silently, the boys fell in behind them.

Turn to page 42

42

Because the men weren't aware of the Hardys' presence, the brothers were able to get close enough to overhear their conversation.

"The girl is Nancy Drew," the taller one said. "Griffin must have contacted her again after we chased him out of the truck stop in River Heights."

The smaller man rubbed his chin. "He's already delivered the goods. Let's take them both now. That way they won't be around to interfere when the 'fireworks' start. Ha ha ha!"

Frank touched Joe's arm. "I wonder what they're up to?" he whispered.

Turn to page 53

43

They decided to search for the *Greenglobe*.

"But where?" Frank asked. "It could be anywhere on the ocean."

"Why don't we try the bay?" Nancy suggested. "It's a start." She turned the plane and headed for Bayport Bay. Soon a white sailboat appeared on the water, anchored, and illuminated by moonlight.

"There she is," Frank announced as Nancy made a low pass over the boat. "But she seems to be abandoned!"

"Let's land and then take out the *Sleuth* to see what's going on," Joe suggested.

A short while later the Hardys' sleek speedboat was moored alongside the silent *Greenglobe*. The young detectives boarded the big boat and were stunned by what they found. A dozen large black oil drums were stacked amidships, and lying bound and gagged at their base was Layne Griffin.

"There's a bomb aboard," he shouted the instant his gag was off. "Those drums are filled with deadly toxic wastes. It's a plot to blackmail Chris Todd."

Turn to page 46

44

The thugs the youths had preceded to Brill's Landing waved to the *Greenglobe*'s captain. He returned the signal and stepped off the boat to join them. Unfortunately, one of the men saw Layne in the crowd. "The truck driver!" he exclaimed.

The captain ran for the *Greenglobe*, and the other three dispersed. Frank, Nancy, and Layne chased the men, each neatly tackling one before the criminals could get away.

The captain had run to the open sail-locker hatch and was waving a signal flare gun over his head. "Don't anyone try to get me or I'll fire a flare into ten drums of explosive toxic waste. Nobody within five miles will be safe."

Just then, Joe climbed out of the hatch. He tackled the captain from behind, knocking the flare gun into the water. Then he held the criminal prisoner with a tight armlock.

Half an hour later the gang was taken away by the police. Frank, Joe, and Nancy waved good-bye to their new friend, Layne, who headed his big rig toward the highway to go home.

"I'm glad we solved the mystery of the secret cargo," Nancy mused. "It makes the world a safer place to live in."

END

45

Joe clambered out the window and hurried to the house. He paused at the door and listened, but heard nothing. Cautiously, he stepped inside. Just as he entered the hallway, a young man with handsome good looks and dark curly hair came out of a room to the right.

Joe froze. Then he saw his brother and Nancy behind the stranger.

"It's okay," Frank said. "This is Layne Griffin. Layne, this is my brother, Joe."

After the two young men had shaken hands, Layne said, "I'm not a very good investigator, Joe. As soon as I tried to open my truck, the men who were following me jumped me and forced me to drive here. They have another truck to haul the cargo to the *Greenglobe*, where I was scheduled to take it. But I suppose they didn't want me to drive all the way to the East Coast once I got suspicious. They were probably afraid I'd manage to attract someone's attention to their scheme. I still don't know what it's all about."

"I do," Joe said. "They're shipping contraband on the *Greenglobe* to Bermuda. From there it will be picked up by someone else. And I'm sure they don't leave witnesses."

"Right! Especially not nosy kids like you!" barked a gruff voice from the door.

Turn to page 52

46

He led the investigators to a crude bomb rigged among the barrels, and Joe safely disarmed it.

"The men who were following me did it," Layne explained. "They forced me to load the drums I was carrying on the boat, then they tied me up and sailed out here. They set the bomb to go off via remote control from the Seneca Hotel, where they're staying. They intend to blow up the ship if Chris Todd doesn't give up his anti-pollution campaign. The explosion would send a deadly cloud of toxic fumes over Bayport."

Nancy was angry. "Obviously they don't care about the environment or people's lives. But with the bomb disarmed, we can go to the authorities and tell them about this awful blackmail scheme. The culprits will be caught thanks to Layne's concern."

"And your excellent detective work," Layne added. "My Greenglobe note was your only clue."

Frank radioed the Coast Guard from the *Sleuth* to retrieve the *Greenglobe* as the three detectives and their new friend motored leisurely back to shore, pleased with what each of them had done to end a dangerous threat to Bayport.

END

47

"Locating a sailboat on the sea at night, even a big one like the *Greenglobe*, is almost impossible," Frank concluded. "Let's see what we can find on the ground."

Soon they landed at Bayport Airport, and a short taxi ride later the determined detectives were at Pier Six, staring at the empty slip where the *Greenglobe* had been berthed earlier.

"There's the phone booth Layne must have been calling from," Joe pointed out. "Let's take a look."

As they scoured every inch of the booth searching for clues, Nancy repeated Layne's desperate words spoken just before he was cut off. "There's danger— somebody coming—phone booth, Pier Six, look up."

Frank stopped his search. "Look *up?*" he said quizzically. "I thought he said, 'Look *out.*'" With that, his eyes darted to the ceiling of the tiny phone booth. "Look up is what he said all right. See?"

Stuck in a grimy corner was a scrap torn from a cardboard box. Frank retrieved it and read the bright red letters printed on it. "EXPLOSIVES!"

Turn to page 57

48

The sleuths watched through the window as Layne got into his truck and the men climbed into their black sedan. A moment later they all drove out of the parking lot and entered the highway.

"We'll have to stay on their trail," Frank said as he opened the door to leave the diner.

Joe was reading a notice posted on a bulletin board by the door. It was another flyer for Chris Todd's concert tour with a list of the towns to be visited. "I'm not sure we have to follow them," he said and pointed out to his companions what he had discovered.

A small, handwritten X was marked alongside one of the towns, and after it were the initials LG. "This message was left for us by Layne," he said excitedly. "And it means he's going to Falls Glen!"

"We can take the back roads and be there before the truck and the sedan arrive!" Nancy declared. "This way we won't risk being seen by his shadows, either."

Minutes later they were driving toward the small town of Falls Glen.

Turn to page 54

Frank nodded and wrinkled his nose. "I wonder what's in this locker," he said. "It smells awfully bad."

Joe bent down to the crack between the door and the floor. "Whew!" he said. "You're right! Must be a dead rat in there. Let's get out of here."

Moments later the Hardys were back on deck. All the tourists were gone because visiting hours were over. A sailor with a red beard stopped the boys. "If you're lookin' for the captain, he's forward," he said, pointing to a tall, gaunt man on the foredeck who shouted orders to the crew. "Is one of you the lad lookin' to ship out with us to Brill's Landing?"

Joe winked secretly to Frank. "Er, yes, I am," he said quickly.

As they walked forward, Joe whispered, "I'll stay on as crew to the next port of call. You get Nancy and meet me there."

Frank nodded approval of the plan.

Joe's knowledge of sailing convinced the captain to hire him to replace a crewman who'd just quit that morning.

To stay with Joe, turn to the next page.
To go with Frank, turn to page 59.

50

Soon the *Greenglobe* was on the open ocean, heading up the coast to Brill's Landing.

Joe busied himself with chores. He liked the sea, and his skills as a sailor made the work a pleasure. But he didn't forget that his real job was to investigate the connection between the *Greenglobe* and Layne Griffin's secret cargo.

I have to learn what's in that sail locker, he thought as he ambled to the rear of the boat. He stopped at the closed hatch directly over the suspicious locker. His nose twitched uncomfortably. "There's that smell again," he gasped.

"Hey, you! Don't you have anything better to do than stand around?" It was the red-bearded sailor. He joined Joe at the sail-locker hatch. Before he could say another word, the strange odor caught his attention, too. "Ugh! Something's been down there since we got the new captain," he said, pointing at the hidden sail locker beneath their feet. "And nobody knows what it is."

Turn to page 58

51

But someone had heard. Before Joe could climb out the window, he was grabbed by the arm, spun around, and forced against the wall. A large man with a dark hat pulled down over his forehead glared at the startled young detective.

"Don't move a muscle," the man warned in a threatening voice that indicated he meant business. Then he called to his accomplices by the two trucks. "We've got a visitor."

In seconds, Joe was surrounded by three grim-faced men in hats.

"You're in a heap of trouble, son," the steely eyed man who'd caught him said between tightly clenched teeth.

For a sudden, surprise ending, turn to page 87.
To pursue the case further, turn to page 64.

52

The startled youths turned and stared into the grim faces of the three unsavory-looking characters they'd only glimpsed up till now. Deep frowns creased the men's faces. One carried a gun. The four young persons knew at once that Joe's estimation of them was correct. They would leave no witnesses to their scheme.

The men forced the detectives and Layne to the backyard of the old farmhouse, where an open well yawned darkly from amid a clump of tall weeds. "It won't get you to China, but it'll get you out of our hair," the thug with the gun chortled. He grabbed Nancy by the arm and forced her to the edge of the well. "Jump, sister," he ordered.

Nancy went limp as if she'd fainted, falling in a heap at the man's feet.

Frank and Joe knew instantly that Nancy's stout heart was not given to faints and picked up her signal. They turned on the men like a well-drilled karate team and lashed out with swiftly flailing chops as Nancy, far from unconscious, grabbed the gun before she pinned her attacker to the ground.

Layne, initially stunned by the suddenness of the action, joined the fray. In seconds, the three thugs were prisoners.

Turn to page 66

After walking some distance, Nancy was just about to turn around, when suddenly a third man sprang from behind a bush and grabbed her. He put a hand to her mouth before she could cry for help. She realized he must be the third man she had seen in the black car the previous day.

Layne raced to Nancy's side, but he was overpowered by his two shadows before he reached her.

"Both of you come with us!" the leader of the men hissed, and he and his partners quickly shoved Nancy and Layne ahead of them.

Joe wanted to come to their rescue, but Frank held him back. "We can get them out of this if things get hairy," the older Hardy decided. "Meanwhile, let's wait and see if they'll lead us to the root of this mystery!"

Turn to page 67

54

When they arrived, Nancy drove to a spot where the main highway entered the town and parked where the detectives could not be seen by incoming traffic.

"Layne should be coming any moment," she said, glancing at her watch.

Sure enough, the big rig appeared several minutes later. Layne drove straight past the hidden youths, not knowing they were there, and headed for the center of town. The black sedan was right behind him.

"Let's follow them," Frank urged. "If we lose them, we won't know where to find them again."

Trailing the two vehicles at a safe distance, the detectives drove to a lovely, open square bordered by grand trees. In the center stood a bandstand surrounded by hundreds of folding chairs. A bright banner flapping in the breeze announced, CHRIS TODD GREENGLOBE BENEFIT CONCERT SUNDAY AFTERNOON. Layne stopped on the street across from the bandstand. The black sedan drove on by and disappeared.

Turn to page 56

The following morning the five friends gathered at Nancy's house. The girl detective made a phone call to Griffin Motorways headquarters, shushing everyone when a man on the other end answered. "Do your trucks go to Barton Falls, Amesbury, Westbury Center, Doddville, Freehoke, and River Heights?" she asked in a pleasant, businesslike manner.

The others were buzzing with excitement when Nancy hung up the phone. "Well? What was the answer?" George Fayne asked.

"Griffin Motorways delivers to all the towns on Chris Todd's concert schedule!" Nancy announced.

Frank was grinning broadly. "Then I know where we can find Layne Griffin!" he said and produced the flyer, holding it for the others to see.

Turn to page 68

56

A short while later the investigators saw three men in dark green worker's coveralls approach the Griffin Motorways truck. One gave Layne a paper to sign, then the three began to unload a number of large cardboard boxes from the back of the rig. They stacked them on the lawn in front of the bandstand. Bright green lettering printed on the boxes said, GREENGLOBE.

"Do you think those men work for Chris Todd's campaign?" Joe asked.

"I doubt it," Nancy replied. She studied the men closely. "They're the same guys who've been following Layne's truck," she announced. "I guess Layne didn't recognize them in those green coveralls."

The sleuths remained in hiding as the men unpacked the cardboard cartons after Layne had driven off. They were filled with hundreds of smaller boxes, also labeled GREENGLOBE. The men placed one small box on each of the chairs in front of the bandstand.

Nancy sniffed the air. "Soap," she determined. "Those containers are filled with soap!"

Turn to page 61

Nancy and Joe stared at the bit of paper in Frank's hand. A portion of a packing label was glued to the tatter of cardboard. On one line were the letters "Gri" and below that on another line was a single letter "M." The rest was torn away.

"Griffin Motorways!" Joe said excitedly. "Layne tore this from one of the boxes he was carrying to tell us what the secret cargo is."

"Why would anyone ship explosives to a boat with a peaceful intent?" Nancy wondered.

"We've got to find that boat," Frank interjected. "Layne said there was danger and now we know why. The *Greenglobe* is carrying a load of explosives!"

"She's gone back to sea," Nancy declared. "But we don't know how long ago she left, or in which direction she's heading. Without that information we'll never find her."

"Storm Larson, the harbor master, may be able to help us," Joe suggested.

Turn to page 70

58

Joe looked puzzled. "If it's been there so long, why doesn't somebody do something about it?"

The sailor shook his head. "Can't. New captain put the sail locker off limits the first day he came aboard."

After he walked away, Joe studied the hatch. What could be down there? he wondered, his interest growing greater by the minute. And does whatever it is have anything to do with Layne's mysterious cargo? As soon as it's dark, I've got to go down there and find out, he concluded.

That night, as the *Greenglobe* headed for Brill's Landing, Joe slipped below decks and made his way forward to the sail locker. He tried the handle. It still would not budge.

The young detective was not aware that a black shadow had followed him silently. Suddenly, without warning, he was hit on the head with a sharp blow. Unconscious, Joe crumbled to the floor.

Turn to page 72

Once on shore, Frank immediately called Nancy's home. "Joe shipped out on the *Greenglobe* as crew," he told his friend. "Her next port of call is Brill's Landing, which is north of here. We're to meet him there. Can you get here by tomorrow morning?"

"Sure," Nancy said. "See you then."

When the girl detective arrived in Bayport, Frank picked her up at the airport, and then the two immediately started up the coast to Brill's Landing. On the way, they stopped for a snack along the highway. When they pulled into the parking lot of a roadside diner, Nancy suddenly pointed to a large black-and-silver truck. "Frank! Look, it says Griffin Motorways on it. I'll bet it's Layne's rig!"

Her eyes searched the area for the familiar black sedan. "Sure," she said after a moment. "Over there is the car that shadowed him before. But no one is in either the truck or the sedan."

"None of these people has seen me before," Frank said. "Do you want me to go into the diner and look around?"

"Maybe—" Nancy began, but was interrupted when three men with hats pulled over their eyes emerged from the diner.

Turn to page 60

59

60

"Those are the people who were shadowing Layne!" Nancy said excitedly.

Two of the men boarded the rig, while the third climbed into the black sedan. A moment later, the truck with the car behind it entered the highway.

"I wonder where Layne is," Nancy said worriedly.

"Maybe we'll find out if we follow those guys," Frank said and moved out of the parking lot. As he passed the spot where the truck had been parked, his nose twitched. "That's the same smell I noticed on board the *Greenglobe*," he said. "And it's also proof that there's a connection between the boat and the secret cargo on that truck."

Many miles down the road the truck parked off the highway in a little-used rest area, and the black sedan moved in behind it. Frank stopped on the shoulder of the road, where he and Nancy could watch the scene from a safe distance.

The men opened the rear of the truck and pulled out an inert form.

"It must be Layne!" Nancy exclaimed, worried.

Turn to page 62

61

The sleuths strolled over to the men, and Frank picked up one of the small green boxes. "Crystal Clear Laundry Detergent," he read aloud. "For a Really Clean Environment."

"Chris Todd would never use his campaign to promote a commercial product!" Nancy snapped. "Do you people work for him?"

"Nope," one of the men replied. "We work for the Crystal Clear Soap Company. Our boss told us to give out these samples before the concert. They came on the truck that just left. Here's the shipping order." He showed the young detectives a paper that read, DELIVER SAMPLES TO FALLS GLEN.

"We'll catch up with Layne and tell him about this dishonest advertising scheme," Joe decided. "Then we'll inform Chris Todd so he can put an end to it."

"I thought I could ditch those guys who were following me when I was at the truck stop," Layne explained later when he had sodas and ice cream with the young people. "But I was in such a hurry that all I could leave Nancy was the Greenglobe clue. Later, I met a state-police friend of mine and gave him the message for Nancy to meet me at 66, hoping I'd be able to talk to her there. But even though I hadn't been aware of it, those guys were still following me and walked in before you people did. All I could do was stick the program on the bulletin board, hoping you'd get the message."

Joe grinned. "We sure did."

END

62

The men lugged the body into the woods. They emerged a few moments later and drove off in the two vehicles.

"Come on!" Frank said and he and Nancy rushed into the dense shrubbery. It was not long before they found the bound trucker.

"Layne!" Nancy cried out.

"Nancy Drew?" Layne moaned as the girl untied him. Then he rubbed a lump on his head.

Quickly Nancy introduced Frank and explained how the Greenglobe clue had helped the investigators.

"I'm glad you found me," Layne said. "I wanted to know what I was carrying, so I opened my truck. I thought I had ditched those guys who were following me, but suddenly they came out of nowhere and knocked me out."

"What was the cargo?" Frank asked.

"Toxic waste," Layne grimaced. "Someone is using my dad's trucks to get rid of deadly poisonous chemicals."

"That explains that awful smell," Frank concluded.

"And it also explains why the *Greenglobe* is involved," Nancy added. "She carries the wastes out to sea where they're dumped. It's a clever scheme. Nobody would suspect Chris Todd's boat's being used for that purpose."

Turn to page 65

64

The men dragged the struggling young detective to the old farmhouse. With Joe as their hostage, Frank and Nancy had to surrender to the criminals. The young investigators were tied securely and thrown down a dark stairway into a pitch-black basement beneath the house.

"That'll keep 'em," one of the men said as they left the youths trapped in the damp, dungeonlike chamber.

"Who's here?" a weak voice called from the darkness.

Nancy and the Hardys gasped. There was another person in the dark room with them!

Turn to page 94

Soon the three were back on the trail of the stolen truck and its load of deadly chemical cargo.

"We have to find out who on the *Greenglobe* is betraying Chris Todd's clean-environment campaign," Nancy said.

"When Layne's rig pulls into Brill's Landing, where the *Greenglobe* will dock, whoever is responsible will go meet her. We've got to be there when he does," Frank said.

With Frank navigating, Nancy drove over narrow backroads to reach the truck's destination before it did. Within a few hours, the three youths were at Brill's Landing, where the *Greenglobe* was tied up, already open for visitors.

"There's Joe," Nancy whispered to Frank as she and the two young men joined a crowd of tourists walking aboard.

Joe saw them and quickly signaled a silent warning to them.

"Act as if you don't know him," Frank ordered. "He must have learned something."

Suddenly, the deep exhaust noise of Layne's rig broke the calm as the huge truck pulled onto the dock, followed by the black sedan.

"Get ready," Nancy warned.

Turn to page 44

66

The youths herded their prisoners to Layne's truck, and trussed them like cattle headed for market. "They'll be safe back there while I drive them to town," Layne said. "The police can take over then."

"We'll notify the FBI, who'll be very interested to hear about this bunch," Frank said as the sleuths walked to Nancy's car.

Later, at the FBI office, federal agents praised the young people for their daring capture of the high-tech smuggling ring. "The gang was shipping sensitive equipment destined for foreign countries through unsuspecting trucking companies and then aboard innocent-looking boats like the *Greenglobe*," an agent explained. "Luckily, Layne here had the good judgment to suspect something and seek your help."

"And the good fortune to get help from Nancy and the Hardys," Layne added with a grin.

END

The Hardys kept a safe distance behind the group. This, however, proved to be the wrong decision. Suddenly, the men pushed Nancy and Layne into a speedboat docked at a lonely pier, and before Frank and Joe could prevent them, they had the engine started and guided the boat away from the dock!

"Where are you taking us?" Nancy demanded.

"For a midnight swim!" the leader chortled.

"Who are you?" Layne asked. "You've been following me since I loaded my truck. I've already delivered the cargo to the *Greenglobe*. What more do you want with us?"

"I suppose it won't hurt to let you know what you were carrying in that rig of yours," the leader replied. "Now that you'll never be able to tell anyone about our scheme, that is!" He grinned evilly in the soft glow of the boat's running lights.

Turn to page 74

68

"These are the towns Chris Todd hasn't visited yet," he said, pointing to the schedule, "the next performance will be in Millwood."

"And you think that's where Layne Griffin is?" Bess asked.

"I'm almost certain. But the easiest way to find out is to ask someone." Frank dialed Griffin Motorways. "One of your drivers is a good friend of mine," Frank said politely, "but I haven't been able to locate him. Can you tell me where Mr. Layne Griffin will be stopping next?

"Millwood!" Frank shouted after he hung up. "Layne is due there this morning."

"Let's go talk to him," Joe suggested eagerly.

Nancy held back. "I still think somebody should keep an eye on Billy John, the drummer."

"Good idea," Frank said. "Do you know where the group is staying?"

"At the Claymore. How about if Bess, George, and Joe pick up Billy John's trail from there, while you and I go to Millwood?"

To go with Frank and Nancy, turn to the next page.
To go with Bess, George, and Joe, turn to page 78.

Nancy and Frank drove to Millwood in Nancy's blue sedan. "This is the only truck stop in town," the girl commented as she pulled off the highway and parked near a small restaurant.

They went inside and Frank spoke to the woman at the cash register. "Have you seen a Griffin Motorways truck lately?"

"Can't say I have," the woman replied. "I wouldn't miss it either, with this big window."

"Thanks," Frank said, and the two friends left. Neither of them had seen two husky men in a booth near the register get up and follow them to the parking lot.

When the detectives got to their car, a young man with dark hair approached them. However, he noticed the two men shadowing them and turned away. A moment later he entered the restaurant.

Nancy realized instantly what had happened. When they climbed into the car, she said excitedly, "Frank, that was Layne Griffin. He recognized me, but then someone scared him away!"

Frank casually glanced out the window. "You're right. There are two men watching us. He must have seen them."

Turn to page 76

70

The sleuths hurried directly to the harbor master's office, which overlooked Bayport harbor with a perfect view of the bay. From it an observer could track every vessel in and out of the busy seaport.

Storm Larson, who knew the young people well, greeted them with a big smile. "What can I do for such famous detectives?" he asked.

The trio explained the importance of locating the *Greenglobe*. "She's been to Bayport a couple of times," the bewhiskered old salt remarked as he searched the pages of his log, where he kept track of all traffic in and out of the harbor. "*Greenglobe . . . Greenglobe . . .* Ah! Here she is. Departed dock at 2230 hours, no destination given."

"That's 10:30 in standard time," Joe said, checking his watch. "It's 11:40 now. We just missed her by 70 minutes!"

Frank stared at the black expanse of water. "She's out there somewhere making no more than eight knots under sail." He turned to his companions. "I think I know how to catch up with her in the *Sleuth* if we hurry."

Turn to next page

The eager detectives thanked Storm Larson for his help and raced to the boathouse, where the *Sleuth* bobbed quietly in the water. Frank and Joe loaded scuba gear for each of the three as Nancy checked the speedboat's fuel and made her ready for sea.

71

Soon the team effort was complete and the sleek speedboat was slapping the black water of Bayport harbor, her sharp prow pointed to sea.

"A large boat like the *Greenglobe* has to stay in the main channel until she reaches the open ocean," Frank called over the roar of the *Sleuth*'s powerful engine. "We can take a shortcut and intercept her before she reaches the end of the channel."

He piloted while Joe and Nancy scanned the horizon with powerful binoculars, searching for the telltale running lights that would identify their quarry. Joe spotted her first. "There she is, one mile dead ahead."

Frank cut the speedboat's engine. "We'll make a half circle around her," he whispered as if the unwary crew on the mystery boat could hear. "Then we'll anchor, put on the scuba gear, and swim up to her in order to board undetected."

Turn to page 84

72

Many hours later, Joe awoke in silent misery inside the dingy, foul-smelling sail locker. A single narrow shaft of dusty light from a crack in the closed hatch above his head enabled him to just barely see.

"Daylight!" Joe muttered, rubbing the painful spot on his head. "I've been out for hours." His senses quickly returned. "The boat's not moving. We've docked!" He stretched to his full height, but he could not see out the crack high above him.

Joe tried the door. It was bolted from the outside, with no keyhole he could pick. He laid his stout shoulder against the door but it was built as strong as the ship. Well, I guess if I can't get out, I might as well do what I came aboard for in the first place—solve this mystery, the determined sleuth thought.

Turn to page 73

As his eyes adjusted to the pale light, he glanced around the small room, seeking a clue to the over-powering stench. He ran his hands along the walls, then dropped to his knees to feel for any possible shred of evidence along the floor. His searching fingers suddenly stopped when they closed around something lying in a corner. Joe raised the object to the shaft of light. A beautiful, coal-black feather with a snow-white tip lay in his open palm. "A bald-eagle feather!" he remarked with astonishment.

As he spoke, the door handle to the locked room began to turn slowly.

73

To see what happens, turn to page 75.
To see what else may happen, turn to page 79.
To find out where the Greenglobe *is docked, turn to page 93.*

74

As the speedboat raced across the bay, the hoodlum described a sinister plot to undermine Chris Todd's clean-environment campaign.

"Everybody in the country knows the *Greenglobe*," he said. "But tomorrow they'll know it even better when pictures of the famous 'clean air' boat are plastered on the front pages of every paper across the nation showing it belching thick, black smoke into the very air Todd says he's going to clean up."

"You're sabotaging Chris Todd's fund drive, which starts tomorrow!" Nancy accused.

"You guessed it," the man responded. "Your trucker friend here just unloaded fifty barrels of polluted fuel for *Greenglobe*'s auxiliary engines that's gonna fill the sky with smelly black smoke when the captain starts them up."

"And people won't believe Chris anymore," Nancy shot back.

"Then our boss can quit worrying about anti-pollution nuts like Todd and go about his business," the man smirked.

The boat drifted to a halt far from shore. Nancy and Layne's ride had come to an end.

Turn to page 77

Joe braced his back against the wall and waited for the door to open.

When it did, a shadowy figure entered the room.

"Frank!" Joe exclaimed.

Frank quickly stepped inside and closed the door behind him. "Shh! I picked the lock. Nobody knows I'm here."

"But how did you find me—?"

Frank put his mouth close to Joe's ear. "We're in Brill's Landing. Nancy's here, too. Layne's truck is near the dock. I came aboard and asked for you. The captain said you'd decided not to ship out and stayed in Bayport. I knew he was lying, so I hid in order to search the boat—" Steps overhead cut Frank's speech short. When they stopped, he continued, "Nancy and I think the *Greenglobe* is secretly shipping something out of the country, but we don't know what—"

This time Joe interrupted, handing Frank the magnificent bald-eagle feather. "It's used by a poaching ring," Joe whispered. "Somebody is transporting killed eagles on Todd's boat—"

Suddenly the boys heard footsteps outside.

Turn to page 86

76

"I have an idea," Nancy said. "Wait here. I'll try to fool these guys." She got out of the car, then called to Frank loud enough to be heard clear across the parking lot, "I forgot to call home. Be right back!"

She went to a nearby phone booth and dialed the number of the restaurant, which she saw on its roadside sign. The cashier answered.

"I'd like to speak with the young man who just came in," Nancy said.

"Just a minute," the cashier replied.

When Layne came on the line, Nancy identified herself, then asked, "Are the two men in the parking lot the reason you walked away from me?"

Layne sounded relieved. "Yes. Those are the guys who've been following me. Sometimes there's a third one."

"Did you make a delivery here in Millwood?"

"How did you know that? I just emptied my truck at the general-shipping dock in town. As a matter of fact, the rig's still there."

"Tell me how to find it, then meet Frank Hardy and me there as soon as you can," Nancy instructed.

"Will do," Layne replied, and gave the young detective directions to the dock.

To go with Frank and Nancy, turn to page 80.
To go to the dock, turn to page 89.

"They've stopped!" Joe said as he watched the thugs' boat from the dock.

"One of the running lights is blinking," Frank noted. "Nancy must be covering it with her hand. Look! She's sending us a message in code!"

Simultaneously, the boys deciphered the blinking signal. "Warn . . . GG . . . do not start . . . sabotage . . ."

"We can't waste any more time!" Frank exclaimed. "I'm going after them in the *Sleuth* while you get Nancy's message to the captain of the *Greenglobe*! Let's move!"

The two brothers parted company. Frank raced to the boathouse where the Hardys' sleek speedboat was docked while Joe hurried toward the *Greenglobe* with Nancy's ominous warning.

To go with Frank, turn to page 81.
To go with Joe, turn to page 83.

78

Later that day, Joe, Bess, and George followed Billy John to Millwood in George's car. Billy John drove to a secluded warehouse and entered. George parked safely out of sight and the three friends kept a watchful eye on the building. Soon another car arrived and two men got out. They, too, disappeared inside the building.

A short while later, the three men emerged. Billy John waved to his companions and drove off. "Shouldn't we follow him?" George asked anxiously.

Joe shook his head slowly. "I want to see what these other two guys are up to," he answered.

Within minutes, Layne Griffin's truck appeared. The men got in their car and Layne followed them up a narrow road into the surrounding hills. As Joe and the girls set out after them, Frank and Nancy showed up in Nancy's sports sedan. "Billy John took off," Joe shouted to Frank. "I'll follow him."

Frank and Nancy grinned. "You won't have to," Nancy called. "He'll be back. Follow us."

Puzzled, Joe said nothing as George pulled in behind the blue sedan. Soon they reached a desolate area stacked high with leaking black drums of toxic chemicals. "A toxic-waste dump!" Joe exclaimed.

Turn to page 113

Joe clenched his fists, ready to defend himself as the door slowly swung open. Then he relaxed. "Frank!" he exclaimed in a low tone.

Frank Hardy, flashlight in hand, stepped quickly into the tiny room and closed the door behind him. "Nancy's here, too," he whispered. "She's outside keeping an eye on Layne Griffin's truck."

"You found him!"

"Nancy picked up his trail—whew! There's that smell again. I wonder what it is?" Frank winced as he spoke.

Joe held up the feather. "Someone is smuggling eagles on the *Greenglobe*," he told his curious brother. "I think it's the captain because a crewman told me the odor started at the same time the new captain shipped on."

Frank rubbed his jaw pensively. "That explains something I just noticed on the dock. Let's get out of here and I'll show you."

Turn to page 100

80

"We have to go back to River Heights right away," Nancy shouted as she returned to her car, making sure the two men could hear every word.

Then she got behind the wheel and started toward her hometown, watching the rear-view mirror to see if the suspects were following. They weren't.

"I think they're glad we're leaving," Nancy laughed. The instant the road behind her was clear, she turned onto a side road. "I watched those guys while you were on the phone," Frank said. "They got into a green truck parked nearby. Whom did you call?"

Nancy told Frank about her conversation with Layne.

"So Layne's mystery cargo is right here in town waiting for someone to pick it up, eh?"

"Exactly. And I think we're going to find out who—and why—by going to the shipping dock."

Turn to page 91

Soon Frank was beating over the waves toward the kidnappers' boat. "I hope I'm not too late," he said as he cut the *Sleuth*'s throttle, slowing her engine to a purr.

The speedboat holding Nancy and the young trucker prisoner bobbed in the darkness. Frank stopped the *Sleuth* some distance away and quietly dropped anchor. He slipped into a wet suit, climbed overboard, and swam with strong strokes toward the other boat.

Nancy and Layne had stalled the thugs as long as they could by pleading for their lives. For a while, the satanic leader of the group let them go on and seemed to take pleasure in their predicament. But finally he shrugged. "We're wasting time," he said. "Say good-bye to each other. It's Davy Jones's locker for you now." With that, he grabbed Nancy to push her overboard.

Layne stepped forward defiantly. His fists were clenched tightly and the muscles in his strong arms rippled with anger. "Get your hands off her—"

Suddenly, the boat tipped sharply. Frank was violently rocking it back and forth with all his might. *"Jump!"* he shouted. With a powerful heave, he flipped the boat over as Nancy and Layne dove neatly into the ocean. The three surprised criminals clung to the boat as it turned turtle.

Turn to page 82

82

Frank, Nancy, and Layne swam safely to the *Sleuth* and climbed aboard. The thugs hung desperately to their overturned boat, shouting for help.

"I'll radio the Coast Guard to pick them up," Frank said with satisfaction. "But first we have to see if Joe got the message to the *Greenglobe* all right."

"Yes," Nancy said. "Layne's cargo was polluted fuel that the crooks dumped into the *Greenglobe*'s tanks to discredit Todd's message to preserve a clean environment."

Frank nodded grimly. "That figures."

Luckily, Joe had been successful. When the trio arrived at the sailboat, the captain thanked the young detectives and their new friend for preventing an unwelcome bit of bad publicity.

"We always burn non-polluting fuel," he told the youths. "Those thugs switched barrels hoping we'd have our picture taken belching black smoke into the sky. Thanks to you and your diligent and dangerous investigation, tomorrow's papers will have pictures of *Greenglobe*'s real message—clean air!"

END

As soon as Joe had warned the *Greenglobe*'s captain not to start the boat's engine, he called Chief Collig of the Bayport Police Department. He explained what happened. "Please come to the docks at once," he urged. "Nancy and Layne Griffin are in extreme danger."

83

A short while later, Joe was on one of a half-dozen fast police boats converging on the surprised hoodlums who held his two friends captive. Frank, in the *Sleuth*, joined the police and pulled alongside the criminals' boat. The startled gang was quickly arrested.

Later, at a dockside café, the young sleuths and their new friend Layne Griffin talked over their exciting case. Layne had dropped the Greenglobe clue for Nancy after he had left their table at the restaurant in such a hurry. He had wanted to write more, but was prevented by the men who were following him.

"I tried to ditch them, but couldn't," he explained.

"Well, I'm glad you were able to finish your second note," Joe said.

"Even though we had a little trouble figuring out what GG meant," Nancy added with a smile.

END

84

A short while later, the *Sleuth* lay at anchor in the darkness less than a quarter of a mile ahead of the slow-moving sailboat. The three detectives were in coal-black wet suits, which blended into the night to make them nearly invisible. They slipped over the side of the motionless speedboat and began swimming strongly toward the *Greenglobe*.

Soon they reached the sailboat. They grabbed a dangling line and quietly hoisted themselves to the deck, where only the helmsman was on duty. The sleuths stowed their tanks in the dim glow of the boat's red and green navigation lights and quietly crept to a porthole in the deckhouse. Nancy peered inside.

Tied in a chair was the missing truck driver, Layne Griffin! In front of him stood a mean-looking man with a shiny bald head. "It's too bad you were so nosy," he said. "Now you'll have to go down with the others when we blow up the *Greenglobe*."

Turn to page 99

86

Before the boys could prepare to defend themselves, the door flew open, and the captain, scowling sharply in the darkness, burst in. He grabbed Frank in a deadly hammerlock before the boy could move. "Don't try anything or I'll break his neck!" he snarled at Joe.

The younger Hardy knew the man meant it. Helplessly, he watched as the captain bound and gagged Frank. When he turned to do the same to Joe, however, the boy attacked. A short fight ensued, but Joe had not recovered from being knocked out earlier and was no match for the strong captain, who subdued him with another blow on the head and trussed him, but not as tightly as he had tied Frank.

"As soon as I've stowed the latest truck-load of eagle carcasses in here and we're on the way to the islands to sell them, you nosy kids can take whatever you've learned to the bottom of the sea with you," the captain sneered. Then he went out, slammed the door behind him, and locked it.

Turn to page 90

But suddenly and unexpectedly, he released his grip! "Why, you're Joe Hardy!" he exclaimed.

Joe stared at his captor in confusion. "Who are you?"

"Agent Harkness of the FBI," the man introduced himself. "These are my colleagues. Now, would you tell me what Fenton Hardy's son is doing here?"

"I'm investigating a case with my brother Frank and Nancy Drew," Joe explained. "At least we thought we were on a case, but now I'm not so sure." He shook his head as he glanced at the identification badge the agent handed him.

Just then Nancy, Frank, and Layne Griffin walked up to the window.

"Come on in," Joe waved and introduced the FBI men.

The young people entered through the barn door. "We found Layne in the house," Frank said, "and thought we'd come to help you in the barn, but it seems you have things under control."

"You walked right into the middle of our Operation Greenglobe," Agent Harkness said with a smile.

"Greenglobe!" the astounded youths chorused.

"Do you mean the note I found at the truck stop wasn't referring to Chris Todd's boat or clean-environ ment campaign?" Nancy inquired with surprise, and showed the agent her clue.

Turn to page 88

88

"No," Harkness replied. "That's an identifying sticker we put on trucks innocently involved in a smuggling operation we're breaking up. It must have fallen off at the truck stop. But why are you involved in this case?"

Nancy and the boys quickly explained the situation.

"I guess we chose a name for our operation that someone was already using," Agent Harkness said. He explained the FBI's plan to stop the illegal export of high-technology equipment to foreign powers. "Until we find out who's behind this scheme, we simply intercept trucks like Layne's here and take the equipment back."

"Well, you sure scared me," Layne said. "I was going to ditch you when I saw you at the truck stop and call Nancy later, but you guys were too good."

The agents accepted the compliment. "Speaking of good investigators, you sleuths aren't so bad yourselves," Agent Harkness said.

With their own case closed, the young people and their new friend Layne Griffin were sworn to secrecy not to reveal Operation Greenglobe, and, of course, they never did.

END

Layne was waiting for Nancy and Frank when they arrived at the general-shipping dock, and pointed out the large crates he had unloaded earlier. "My instructions were to leave them here," he said. "And you see that sedan over there? The two guys that were at the diner left ahead of me and are here now."

The men didn't move. Their eyes were fixed on the unattended crates. A moment later, a truck appeared. Its driver loaded the crates onto his truck, then drove off. But when a blue Ford slipped in behind the truck and followed it toward the highway, the men in the sedan got out of their car and walked directly toward the astonished youths!

Turn to page 116

90

Nancy, meanwhile, had mingled with a group of tourists visiting the famous boat on the open deck above the imprisoned sleuths. Though she pretended to be interested in the *Greenglobe*, she was searching for Frank, who she knew was aboard, and Joe, who was supposed to be aboard. But there was no trace of either of her good friends.

Finally, a brass bell clanged loudly, indicating the end of visiting hours, and a sailor announced, "All ashore!"

I need more time, Nancy thought frantically. Something has happened to them. . . . Her sharp eyes spotted a flicker of light coming from the sealed hatch at the bow. Then she realized that someone was flashing a message in code. Frank and Joe must be in there! she thought.

A sailor took her gently by the arm. "I have to ask you to leave," he said.

Nancy's eyes stayed on the rapidly flickering light coming through the crack in the hatch cover. "N . . . We are both trapped . . . F and J."

"Please, miss, you have to leave now," the sailor repeated.

Nancy pulled free from his grip and raced to the hatch cover. "Frank! Joe!" she shouted. "I'm coming!"

Turn to page 95

Nancy quickly circled back to the truck stop. The green truck had just pulled out of the parking lot and was driving toward town. Layne had started walking, and she picked him up on the way.

"Hop in!" she called out.

The young man climbed into the back seat and Nancy continued her pursuit of the green truck.

It entered Millwood and, as she expected, proceeded directly to the general-shipping dock, where Layne had unloaded his cargo, a stack of black oil drums.

The men got out and quickly lifted the drums onto their truck. Then they drove off.

The blue sedan followed at a safe distance, unseen by the suspects.

Turn to page 92

92

The green truck headed to the outskirts of Millwood and vanished into a thick woods. When the road became very narrow, Nancy, Frank, and Layne stopped their car and hopped out.

"We'll follow them on foot," Frank decided. "Come on, I'm sure they can't go far on this road."

The trio ran through the brush, listening to the sound of the truck's exhaust. Suddenly, the woods were silent. The truck had stopped in a clearing just beyond a small knoll. When the young detectives got there, they hid behind bushes at the edge of the open area and watched the men unload the barrels.

"They'll leave as soon as they've finished dumping that stuff," Nancy predicted. "Frank, why don't you and Layne hide our car, then come back here."

The two young men ran off to camouflage the sedan so the suspects would not see it on their way back.

To stay with Nancy, turn to page 97.
To go with Frank and Layne, turn to page 98.

93

A moment later the door opened and Joe was confronted by the *Greenglobe*'s captain, who was brandishing a heavy club. "You can shout for help if you like, you meddler," he snarled. "But there's nobody else on the boat but you and me—and in a minute there'll just be me."

"You're smuggling eagles," Joe accused him, waving the beautiful feather he'd found.

"So what?" the captain spat back. "There's plenty of them."

"They're an endangered species and they're also our national bird. It's illegal to hunt, kill, or sell them," Joe shouted.

"Who cares? I get plenty to ship to the Caribbean Islands, where the natives use them to make fake Indian headdresses," the captain responded. He raised the club, ready to hit Joe, when he suddenly dropped to the floor like a stone.

Joe shook his head in disbelief as a man stepped from the shadows behind the fallen captain. With him were Frank and Nancy. "It's okay, son," the man said. "I'm with the National Park Service, and our friend here has just been tranquilized by a small missile from this dart gun. He'll recover in plenty of time to stand trial for his deeds, thanks to the help of you three investigators and Layne Griffin."

Turn to page 109

94

"Who are you?" Nancy asked, almost certain she recognized the voice. "Layne?"

"Yes," Layne replied. "Is that you, Nancy?"

"Yes. It's me and the Hardy boys. What happened?" Nancy inquired eagerly as she and the Hardys worked to free their hands.

"I was supposed to deliver those crates to the *Greenglobe*, in Portsmouth," Layne explained. "But I knew there was something fishy about the whole operation. When the men showed up in the restaurant where I was talking to you, I tried to ditch them, figuring I could call you later. I started to write a note, but they captured me and brought me here. They're going to transfer the cargo to another truck and deliver it to the *Greenglobe* themselves. They know that because I haven't reported to my dad all day, the police will be looking for me."

"They're using the *Greenglobe* to ship illegal cargo," Nancy reasoned. "But why?"

"Because the boat is going to Bermuda," Joe explained. "From there the stuff will be picked up by someone else, probably a foreign buyer. I overheard the men in the barn say so."

Layne had been working on his own bonds for hours. With a burst of energy, he broke them free. "Let's get out of here!" he exclaimed.

Turn to page 96

Then she raced to the locker where the boys were trapped. Joe had managed to free himself and give the signal, but Frank was still bound. Nancy quickly cut his bonds with a small pocket knife, then the three ran out the door.

The sailor, who had followed the girl in consternation, was stunned to see Frank and Joe emerge. "Your captain is using you and your ship illegally!" Frank told him. "He was smuggling bald-eagle carcasses—that's why the locker smelled so bad!"

With that, the three sleuths ran to the upper deck. The captain realized his scheme was ended as soon as he saw them. He leaped ashore, straight into the arms of Layne Griffin, who tackled him to the ground. Defeated, the captain confessed everything.

"Poachers ship the eagle carcasses to me so I can transport them to islands in the Caribbean where they're made into Indian artifacts. We figured nobody would suspect if I used a boat belonging to a famous environmentalist. My men follow the truckers to make sure they get here."

"They were the guys I saw at the truck stop," Layne said. "I tried to ditch them, hoping I could contact you later, Nancy. I started writing a note telling you where I was headed, but they saw me, so I just threw it on the ground, hoping you'd find it and understand."

"The Greenglobe clue," Nancy said as all the pieces of the investigation fell together. "One simple word that'll put all these thugs in jail."

END

96

Quickly he freed Nancy and the Hardys, and they made their way out of the cellar and raced to the barn. Layne's rig was still there, but the second truck loaded with the illicit cargo was gone.

"How do we get to Portsmouth?" Layne asked.

"We'll have to get the next flight to the East Coast," Frank said. "Come on, let's get our car."

Late the following afternoon the four young people were at the dock where Chris Todd's grand sailboat was berthed. Its decks were filled with tourists.

"There's the truck," Nancy said as the rig with the illicit cargo pulled alongside the dock. Then the three thugs got out and walked to a nearby phone booth.

"If they get those crates loaded and the boat outside the legal limit, nobody can board her to stop that cargo from reaching its destination," Frank said.

"Those crates aren't going anywhere," Layne snapped. "Watch."

The determined youth dashed across the dock to the truck and clambered aboard. He released the parking brake and steered the vehicle toward the water's edge, then leaped to safety.

Turn to page 111

The moment the green truck left the clearing, Nancy hurried to the stack of dumped drums. She read the label pasted on the side of a barrel: HAZARD-OUS CHEMICALS—BEWARE!

97

"A toxic-waste dump!" Frank cried a moment later as he and Layne joined Nancy at the ominous pile of barrels.

"I knew there was something suspicious about this operation when we weren't allowed to see the cargo," Layne commented.

"There's more to it than that," Frank said. "We believe this dumping is linked with Chris Todd's campaign for a clean environment, Greenglobe."

"That's the name I overheard the men who hired our truck say!" Layne exclaimed. "I wrote it down on a slip of paper."

"We found it," Nancy said, and explained to the astonished trucker what they'd learned so far.

"You mean my dad's company has been hauling toxic wastes to these towns without knowing it?" Layne cried angrily.

"Yes," Nancy stated. "The dumps are set up and then 'discovered' just a few days before Chris Todd's concert."

Turn to page 101

98

Layne stopped suddenly as a car approached. "That's the third guy who was following me," he exclaimed.

Frank recognized the man instantly. "It's Billy John, Chris Todd's drummer!" he stated. Then his jaw dropped open in stunned disbelief. Seated beside Billy John was Chris Todd himself!

The singer came to a halt when he saw Layne and the young detectives. "I see you're on to our little scheme," he said, and hung his head. "I suppose the whole thing wasn't such a good idea after all."

"Tell us about it," Frank urged.

"Well, I wanted to get public sympathy for my cause to protect the environment," Chris said. "I had Billy John set up fake toxic-waste sites, which would be discovered just before my concerts. The public would be outraged, of course, and each town we visited would really begin to do something to clean up the environment."

"It was done with the best of intentions," Billy John added.

When the sleuths and Layne Griffin discussed the curious case later, everyone agreed that it was completely unnecessary for Chris Todd to get attention through negative publicity. "The truth is always best," Nancy declared. "It's the one thing everyone can believe in."

END

99

Layne shook his head angrily. "You've already blackmailed Chris Todd into giving up his clean environment crusade. Isn't that enough? Why do you have to destroy the *Greenglobe* and its innocent crew?"

The bald man sneered. "It's the only way Todd will know we're serious so he'll never dare reorganize his stupid campaign."

"I wouldn't be so sure," Layne spat. Even though he faced an untimely end, his spirit was strong and his determination great.

The detectives gathered in a dark corner of the deck. "So that's what's behind this," Frank said. "Somebody wants Chris Todd's clean-environment message stopped."

The clanging of the boat's bell shattered the silence. "Prepare to abandon ship," the bald-headed man shouted, and went up to the helmsman, who lashed the boat's wheel.

Turn to page 103

100

"How'd you know I was in the sail locker?" Joe inquired as he and Frank sneaked off the boat.

"You weren't anyplace else I looked. It had to be either in there or overboard. I had to pick the lock to get you out."

Nancy was hiding behind a stack of crates piled on the dock. "Frank! Joe! Over here!"

The rejoined trio remained hidden as they observed a pack of dogs yelping at Layne's parked truck. "I see what you mean," Joe remarked. "They smell something, and my guess is it's eagle hides."

Frank explained the situation to Nancy. "Someone is buying eagles from poachers and shipping the hides with feathers by truck to the *Greenglobe*'s captain, who probably takes them out of the country to the Caribbean Islands where they're used to make expensive decorative Indian souvenirs. They're extremely valuable. And illegal!"

Just then the captain appeared and Layne began to argue loudly with him at his truck. "I won't unload my cargo unless you tell me what it is," Layne said angrily.

The captain reached ominously into his pocket.

"He may have a weapon," Frank shouted. "Let's get him!"

Turn to page 102

Her eyes gleamed brightly. "I think I have a way to foil this operation."

She explained her plan to Frank and Layne as the three drove into Millwood, where they proceeded to the local newspaper office.

Byron Chippendale, the paper's publisher, greeted the youths. "Your father is a friend of mine, Nancy. Tell me what I can do for you."

Nancy explained the unusual situation. "We think one of Chris Todd's group members is behind the scheme, but we don't have enough evidence to prove it. You see, a few days before a concert, a toxic-waste-dump site is found. Millwood is the next town on the schedule and—"

A brief knock on the publisher's office door was followed by the alarmed entry of Mr. Chippendale's secretary. "An anonymous caller just reported a toxic-waste dump in the woods outside of Millwood," she said breathlessly.

Mr. Chippendale smiled wryly at the youths. "It appears that your conclusions are correct," he said thoughtfully. "Tell me what I can do to help."

Turn to page 106

102

A moment later, the surprised captain was surrounded by the three athletic young detectives, all ready and willing to act if necessary. Realizing he was trapped, the desperate man shoved Joe into Frank and dashed around the front of the truck. But Layne, rushing after him with Nancy, tackled the desperado, who meekly surrendered and confessed.

"So the men who were following me were the captain's cronies," Layne remarked as he enjoyed a soda at a dockside café with Nancy and the Hardys. "I tried to get rid of them at the truck stop, but without success. I didn't even have a chance to finish talking to Nancy."

"The police will pick them up," Joe said. "And federal agents will arrest the poachers who are killing our national bird."

When Layne boarded his truck for his long drive home, the four youths became fast friends, and the case of the secret cargo was a memory they could all share the next time they met.

END

From page 99

103

As the investigators watched, the third man, whom Nancy had seen in the car following Layne, appeared.

"Hank, the *Greenglobe*'s crew is tied below along with that nosy truck driver," the bald man told him. "Set the timer to detonate the explosives in five minutes and get the *Zodiac* ready for sea."

Hank lowered a black rubber boat over the side and then dashed below. "The timer is set," he shouted when he reappeared.

"Get aboard the *Zodiac*," the bald man rasped.

The three men jumped into the rubber boat and their leader piloted it out of the blast area. Then he stopped. "I want to make sure she blows up," he said, his voice drifting over the waves for the young detectives to hear aboard the doomed sailboat.

"We've got to move fast," Frank whispered. "I'll go below and defuse the bomb. You free the crew and get off this boat—just in case I don't succeed."

Knowing they must each work quickly, the friends dove below decks as the timer quietly ticked away the remaining minutes.

To follow Frank, turn to the next page.
To go with Nancy and Joe, turn to page 108.

104

Frank scrambled down the gangway three steps at a time. A crew member lay on the lower deck, his hands and feet tied and a gag in his mouth. Frank tore the gag free. "Where's the bomb?" he demanded as he rapidly untied the surprised man's bonds.

"Below," the man gasped. "Next to the fuel tanks!"

"Help free the others and then get off this boat!" Frank ordered as he disappeared down the stairway.

"Yes, *sir!*" the relieved crewman shouted.

Frank grabbed an emergency flashlight from the wall and cast its beam around the engine room. The light picked out four large cardboard cartons stacked against the fuel tanks. A simple battery-powered clock with two thin wires leading to the cartons told Frank all he needed to know. "The explosives!" he choked. The hands of the clock were less than a minute away from touching. Frank dove across the room for the dangling wires.

To learn immediately if Frank succeeds, turn to page 110.

If you can stand the suspense, turn to page 112.

106

The early-evening edition of the Millwood newspaper was on the streets within an hour. Its headline screamed boldly, TOXIC-WASTE-DUMP REPORT PHONY!

"That should get whoever is behind this scheme into the open," Frank said, reading the story Mr. Chippendale had put in his paper.

"Into the clearing is more like it," Nancy said with a grin.

Frank, Nancy, and Layne immediately drove to the woods. Layne stayed to camouflage the car, while Nancy and Frank hid within sight of the barrels, which were still there.

"If Billy John is the one involved in this operation, as we suspect, he'll be here soon to find out what went wrong," Nancy commented as the youths waited for the rest of her plan to unfold.

A moment later, a car carrying Billy John and the two men from the green truck entered the clearing. "You see? They're right where we dumped 'em, Billy. Just like you told us," one man whined.

"And I told the newspaper where to find the dump, just like I done in all them other towns," the other man said.

Now the youths had all the information they needed to go to the police. But as they started to sneak away, Billy John spotted them. After a brief fight, the young detectives were subdued.

Turn to next page

"So that's why the newspaper article lied," Billy John snarled. "The famous Nancy Drew and the Hardy boys are investigating my scheme, eh? Well, it'll be your last case. Put 'em in the barrels, men."

The men grabbed the youths. "You created these toxic-waste dumps for the publicity, didn't you, Billy?" Nancy accused the drummer.

"It worked, didn't it?" he snapped. "I get a percentage of how much the group earns. My 'toxic-waste dumps' really get the public stirred up. We have sellout crowds wherever we go."

Just then, Layne appeared at the edge of the clearing. Billy John went for him like a flash of lightning and managed to twist the young trucker's hands behind his back. "Interesting," Billy hissed. "I thought Joe Hardy had blond hair."

"He does," a voice from the woods shouted. Joe raced into the clearing and knocked Billy John flat, as Frank and Layne turned on the other two men.

Joe, Bess, and George had followed Billy John from River Heights. The three sleuths and their friends quickly subdued the criminals.

"It was a clever idea," Frank remarked, "but Layne's suspicions and the slip of paper Nancy found were the beginning of its end—and yours."

"And the public doesn't need to be lied to about the dangers to the environment," Nancy added. "The truth is already scary enough!"

END

108

Nancy and Joe freed the grateful crew, who immediately slipped over the side into the life raft and paddled away from the *Greenglobe*, which might explode at any moment. Then the two wet-suited sleuths entered the water and silently swam to the *Zodiac*, where the bald-headed man and his cohorts waited for their evil work to be concluded.

Joe neatly sliced a long cut in the bottom of the air bladders of the rubber *Zodiac*. The craft immediately began to sink.

"Help! I can't swim!" the bald-headed man screamed as he plopped into the water. "Save me!"

"Save yourself," his companions shouted.

But Joe and Nancy were ready. They dragged the leader back to the limp rubber boat and guarded all three men, who clung to the damaged craft like rats to a floating log.

Frank signaled from the *Greenglobe* that all was safe and soon everyone was aboard, the sleuths in complete command of the situation.

Later on shore, the Hardys, Nancy, and their new friend Layne Griffin toasted their success with mugs of hot chocolate as the sun rose over a tranquil Bayport harbor.

END

Later, at a dockside café, the Park Service officer continued his explanation of the case to Nancy, the Hardys, and Layne Griffin, who had joined the group.

"We've been tracking this poaching ring for months. We followed Layne, hoping his shipment would lead us to the person buying the illegal feathers. It did. We decided it was time to move in when we realized Joe might be in danger. You all deserve thanks for outstanding service to your country and its wildlife."

The glow of pride for a job well done lasted long after the Park Service officer had left. The sleuths shook hands with Layne and wished him well, inviting the young trucker to visit any of them the next time he passed through either River Heights or Bayport.

"I hope next time I won't have to run from someone following me as I did at the truck stop," Layne said with a grin. "Or that at least I'll have time to finish writing you a note telling you where I'm going!"

END

110

However, Frank's feet slipped and he fell soundly against the bulkhead, striking his head on a steel pipe!

Frank shook his head. He was stunned by the blow, but he could still see that less than thirty seconds remained before the bomb would detonate.

He struggled to his feet and moved unsteadily toward the dangling wires, his trembling hands reaching out to tear them loose.

His fingers closed around them seconds before the clock's hands touched. He ripped the wires and smashed the clock to bits against the bulkhead. Then he slumped against the fuel tank, his whole body shaking.

The clatter of running feet overhead stirred the groggy youth. "There's a fight on deck!" he cried out. His energy quickly restored by the continuing threat, he clenched his fists and scrambled up the gangway to help his friends.

Turn to page 114

The shocked crowd scattered as the truck dropped off the dock into the water with a loud splash. Soon wooden crates began to bob to the surface.

The startled thugs ran straight into the arms of the four youths, who wrestled them to the ground.

"Call the police," Joe shouted to a surprised on-looker.

After the criminals had confessed and were hauled off to jail, the youths watched as the truck and the spilled cargo were salvaged from the water.

"The smugglers thought nobody would ever suspect that a boat promoting a clean environment would be engaged in an illegal operation," Nancy said. "But they were wrong."

"I'm glad Layne called you," Frank added. "Otherwise the gang might have gotten away with it!"

END

112

The *Zodiac* bobbed on the water a safe distance from the *Greenglobe*. The bald-headed leader looked at his watch. "Something's wrong," he said. "The bomb should have gone off three minutes ago." He glared at the accomplice he'd given the job of arming the bomb. "You oaf. You did something wrong."

The man protested, but it was clear the bomb was not working. "We're going back on board," the leader decided. "Turn about!"

The man steering the bulbous rubber boat stood up quickly. "Not me," he shouted. And without another word, he leaped into the sea.

The two remaining crooks shivered under their leader's scowl. "It might go off when we get aboard," one of them argued.

"It's suicide," the other wailed.

The bald man grabbed the tiller and steered for the *Greenglobe*. "Our job is to stop Chris Todd from spreading his message," he rasped. "Destroying the *Greenglobe* will keep him quiet forever."

The two men glanced at each other, then followed their companion over the side.

"Cowards!" the leader screamed as he raced toward the *Greenglobe*. "I'll blow it up myself!"

Turn to page 115

Suddenly, police cars converged on the site. With the scores of policemen was Billy John, giving orders! The men Layne had followed surrendered without a fight.

Billy John greeted the surprised youths. "I'm an agent with the Environmental Protection Agency. Your excellent detective work helped our effort to expose secret toxic dumps like this. You see, our agency has access to names of illegal dumpers. Another agent working with me contacts them, telling them that he is looking for places to get rid of chemical wastes for clients. Whenever he gets a deal, we ship a load of barrels filled with water to the dumpers. Then they lead us to the dumps, where we find all the evidence to convict them."

"Like today," Frank said with a grin.

"Right."

Layne grinned ruefully. "I wish I'd known what I was getting into ahead of time. Then I wouldn't have panicked at the truck stop and run before I could finish talking to Nancy."

Frank chuckled. "But that would have taken the secrecy out of your 'secret cargo!'"

END

114

When he reached the deck, though, the others had the situation well under control.

The bald-headed man and his evil crew lay in a heap on the floor with Nancy, Joe, Layne, and the *Greenglobe*'s crew standing over them.

"These thugs came back aboard when they saw the crew was free," Nancy explained to Frank. "But we were ready for them."

Joe glanced nervously at his brother. "Er, by the way, you *did* find the bomb, didn't you?"

Frank nodded. "I found it. As for you," he said to the terrified thugs, "you might as well confess whom you're working for, because if you don't, I can always hook the wires back up."

The bald-headed man admitted he and his companions were in the employ of a chemical company, a convicted environment polluter whose management held a grudge against Chris Todd and wanted to end his career.

"I had heard the word 'Greenglobe' mentioned, so I wrote it on a slip of paper when I tried to ditch these guys at the truck stop," Layne explained. "But I didn't know it was the name of Todd's boat. All I knew was that I had to deliver my cargo to Pier Six in Bayport."

The next day the paper announced, CHRIS TODD TOUR TO CONTINUE AS PLANNED—thanks to the diligent efforts of a group of youths interested enough to care.

END

Nancy, Joe, Frank, and the crew of the sailboat waited hidden on deck as the irate crook clambered aboard, muttering under his breath. Frank had the disarmed bomb detonator in his hands. He stepped in front of the startled man. "Is this what you're looking for?" he asked.

The stunned criminal was instantly surrounded and captured, and then his accomplices were retrieved from the ocean. Soon all were imprisoned safely in the sail locker for the ride back to Bayport.

"Chris Todd will reopen his campaign when he learns the *Greenglobe* is safe." Nancy smiled.

Within days, the organizer of the plot was caught as a result of the crooks' confessions. He was a convicted polluter out for revenge on Chris Todd, whose earlier efforts had sent him to jail.

The credit for uncovering the plot and solving the case of the secret cargo was given to the three young detectives and their new friend, Layne Griffin, whose suspicions and a simple, one-word clue, Greenglobe, started it all. They were honored at a gala event sponsored by a grateful Chris Todd.

END

116

"Don't be alarmed," one of them said. "We're government agents and know you have been investigating the Griffin cargo." He gestured toward the unmarked truck vanishing from sight, and the blue Ford following it. "Those crates contain equipment being shipped to a secret laboratory. Even we don't know its location. Our job is to guard the stuff until we pass the duty on to the other agents like those in that car. We knew Layne was suspicious about us, and when you detectives entered the case, we were worried you might upset our undercover mission. Luckily, the cargo is on its last leg and we can all relax."

"But what about Greenglobe?"

The agent smiled at Frank's question. "We planted the note as a false clue to throw off Nancy's investigation. It was a word we saw on a poster."

Just then Joe, Bess, and George arrived, and were introduced to the agents.

"We checked out Billy John," Joe revealed. "All we could find out is that he tried to schedule the concerts in towns that had problems with toxic-waste dumps. He felt it was a good idea to reinforce the publicity the dumping got to make people more conscious of how important a clean environment is."

"It *is* a good idea," Layne agreed.

END